PANGAEA

Where Magic Was Born

Volume 3: The Age of Dark Ages

Roger Schafer

Dedication

I dedicate this book to my family, for always being so supportive, including my grandparents, who have passed away. I thank my friends, some of whom I have known since I was a child, and others who became a part of my life later. All of them are still a part of my life today.

Most of all, I want to thank my parents, Roger and Barbara, along with my two younger brothers, Michael and Daniel. They have been my backbone and support.

Lastly, I dedicate this book to you, the reader. Without you reading my books, this would not be possible. I truly hope you know that I love the support and your wonderful comments on my earlier books. Thank you for buying my books and sharing these stories.

Acknowledgements

I would like to thank my friends and family for their utmost support and faith in me. It is through their love that I was able to make this book a reality. I would also like to thank my publication team for their patience and hard work, especially Irene Pearson for her patience and dedication to my project.

Thank you all.

About the Author

Roger "Derby" Schafer is best known to his family and friends as "Derby." His father's name is Roger and mother's name is Barbara. Derby is the oldest of three and has two younger brothers, Michael Schafer and Danny Schafer. Derby was born in New Mexico and currently lives in Las Vegas, Nevada, where his parents live. Derby's two younger brothers also live in Las Vegas, Nevada.

This is the fifth book published by "Derby" among *The Perfect Season*, *Discovery of Eko and Indra*, *Eko and Indra: The Summer Olympians* Book 2, *Pangaea How Magic Was Born Volume 1 The Origin of Magic*, and *Pangaea How Magic Was Born Volume 2 Pandora's Box*.

Thank you for your support. This book will keep you hooked. Find out in the next book what happens to our hero as the battler of the forces of magic – Light 'Goodness.'

Preface

The Age of Darkness begins from the time when the Monarch King calls upon all the Evil and Darkness in the Galaxy and gives the last command to destroy everything. Pangaea Lia The Canterpillar rises against the Monarch King and attempts to protect all living things. Things that breathe air, creatures that live on the land or in the water, or those in the surrounding ocean, in and around all of Pangaea.

Lia's butterflies strive to protect all living things grown out from under the ground such as grass, wheat, plants, shrubs, trees, bushes, flowers, and weeds. The Goodness and Love of both Lia the Canterpillar and that of the release of the trapped Good "Light" Magic work in unison against the Evil and Darkness.

However, Lia and her butterflies cannot protect everything. The Age of Darkness explains the events that will tell the truth of what happens in the times we know as the Dark Ages. The Age of Darkness reveals many other things in this story, including the forces of Darkness: Erikings, Atlantians, Gargoyles, and those that were not protected by the Butterflies, and many creatures that were not of the Darkness. The Dark Ages also unveils the lives of the Heroes, the Creatures of "Light," bearing Good Magic and a Pure Heart. When necessary, the heroes become the Warriors. Today, they are known as the Six, Saviors of all living things. The Heroes comprise Su the Pixie, Z the Unicorn, Hope the Fairie, Tay the Turtle, Liz the Lizard, Pi the Spider, Ty the Toad, and of course, Lia the Canterpillar.

The events that this story covers take place during the time all life is asleep in hibernation because of the protective Magical Cocoons of the Good "Light," provided by Lia the Canterpillar. The Cocoons attempt to protect all life from the Act, the last Command of the Monarch King to destroy all life in Pangaea. This time period of hibernation and sleep lasts until all creatures begin to wake up. When all life wakes up, millions of years have passed since the final Act of the Monarch King, the King of the Erikings, and the former Ruler of Pangaea. Now, with the protection provided by the Good "Light," the Cocoons, Lia has transformed inside the Good "Light" Magic.

For years, the Good "Light" Magic had been trapped and controlled by the Monarch King and his Warriors: the Erikings, Gargoyles, and Dragons, who are the most powerful of all the Clans, for an untold amount of time. Lia the Canterpillar had been one of the chosen who could touch the Pandora's Box and release the Good "Light" Magic. Using the Good "Light" Magic, trillions and trillions of Butterflies filled with the same Good Magic were able to release the "Light" Good Magic and helped Lia the Canterpillar with protecting most lives.

Lia the Canterpillar was the first and the only creature to touch and provide "Freedom of the trapped Good Magic." Lia was a creature herself, but she was filled with only Light and Goodness being one of the chosen, who were selected by "Su" the Pixie and "Hope" the Fairie as the only creatures capable of opening the Pandora's Box and that released the dormant, trapped "Light" Good Magic to save all life and all creatures in and around all of Pangaea. By this single heroic act, Lia intends to save even those who were on the dark side, such as Erikings, Gargoyles, and any creature that was filled with the Dark "Evil" Magic. Some of the pregnant Erikings, the mothers who had recently given birth to young Erikings as the battle of the North was happening, only survived because of the Butterflies as do the newborn Erikings. These new mothers and the young Erikings that were born as those battles happened were protected by the same Butterflies that protected all other creatures. The same is true for the Dictator, the other Gargoyles, and any other creature that was not at the final battle. They had survived the battles of the North Coast and at the Center of the Erikings' territory where the Good "Light" Magic had been trapped in the Pandora's Box and was being held as a captive.

The Dragons, Yeti, Unicorns, Pixies, Fairies, and all the other lives: Furs, Skins, Hides, and Scales most had protection from Lia's Butterflies and got encased in Cocoons. Some creatures were able to escape to protect themselves from the "Evil" and Darkness summoned by the Monarch King. In his last Command, the Monarch King called upon the "Evil" and Darkness from the entire Galaxy, not only the Darkness from the Planet in order to destroy all life in and around Pangaea. As a last line of defense, Lia's Butterflies intend to protect all life on Pangaea, but they could not.

The Age of Darkness focuses on the Dark Ages when the Planet was in Darkness and in hibernation. In Volume 3 of the series, Pangaea: Where Magic Was Born: The Age of Darkness, you will learn about the damage that life on the planet suffers because of millions of years of hibernation. You will discover what really happened in the Age of Darkness.

Contents

Chapter 1
The Butterfly Effect

After millions of years, our Heroes and all other living things are slowly beginning to awaken now. They are waking up into a new era. Many things have changed while everyone was in hibernation except for the forces of "Evil" and Darkness. What were they doing while all life slept?

In the Age of Darkness, the Darkness prevailed as did the "Light." Both grew as long as they lasted. We know what the Good "Light" Magic was doing, protecting all living and breathing creatures and plants, both on the land and in or beneath the lakes and the surrounding ocean.

We have yet to learn of the Dark "Evil" Magic. What events happened during the Dark Ages? What became of the Erikings, Gargoyles, Atlantians, and other creatures of the Dark nature? What happened during the time of the impact until the Earth healed life and all living creatures, both breathing and growing? With his last dying breath and act, the Monarch King did indeed call for all the Evil "Dark" Magic to destroy all life and the entire planet. But what the

Monarch King was unaware of was that Evil first appeared, and prior to its strike on the planet, it struck the Pandora's Box directly. As it was entering the atmosphere from space, it appeared to be endless. While nearing Pangaea, it got bigger and wider. It struck Pangaea in the exact spot where the Pandora's Box had been held for millions of years under the watchful eye of an Eriking who was called the Monarch King. The force that was called upon to strike Pangaea from the universe was being funneled. It looked like a tornado, but it was far larger than one. It even covered the stars and the lights in the night from the lands of Pangaea.

Pandora's Box is invincible and did not break from the impact. However, the force of the "Evil" from the entire galaxy was so powerful that when it struck the open Pandora's Box, it actually pushed it several miles deep into the planet, creating a large crater in the ground as it went. Due to the sheer force, the dirt that was below was being propelled in all directions creating a life-ending dust storm on all of Pangaea. The dust was a result of the pressure released by the impact because of the power, force, and intensity with which the Darkness had hit Pandora's Box. What once was the Eriking Territory and the areas near or close by were all a part of the ground. If not for the Butterflies, all life on Pangaea would be underground with them.

Everything that the Butterflies touched was saved. The rest was all affected by the impact of the tornado of the Darkness. As the Territory of the Erikings went underground, Pangaea, which had been one planet where all life lived together, broke and divided into the seven continents that the world is today. That was the end of Pangaea the way it had been. All life awoke in a divided land from the hibernation after millions of years because it was encased in the Cocoons by the Butterflies that came to protect all life as Lia the Canterpillar opened the Pandora's Box and released the Good "Light" Magic.

When everything else was in hibernation and asleep, the Dark creatures prayed to the Evil to protect them and take them as loyal servants. They had to survive the destruction of Pangaea in some form or manner, and this was it. Good and Evil are both forces, just like night and day. Just as these forces, so are there "Light" and "Dark" Magic. Even if it was trapped for millions or even billions of years, Magic survived. It is the creator and the destroyer of not only galaxies but the entire universe.

When our heroes began to wake up along with the other survivors of the battles, they assumed that everything was Good and there was no more Evil. However, Evil still lurked in the corners of the Earth.

Evil had grown in the areas the Butterflies had not been present at. The sheer size of Pangaea had not allowed the Butterflies to protect everything on it. Pangaea had deep caves, large oceans, and high mountains. It had volcanoes and forests all over. Even with trillions of Butterflies, there was no way to cover everything.

Life was present in all the areas that were not protected by the Butterflies. Evil "Dark" Magic had taken hold of all the unprotected life to help them survive as Darkness grew. While the Monarch King had control over the Pandora's Box, the "Light" Magic had been trapped inside it. However, when everything that the Butterflies had protected had been in Cocoons, the "Dark" Magic had been free to grow and affect all life outside the Butterflies' protection. It influenced all unprotected life to turn them to the dark side.

Every living creature, Good or Bad, that had managed to stay alive during the hibernation had either been influenced by the dark side or had to fight the growing Darkness to survive. The creatures who were Evil and had been protected by the Butterflies could break out of the Cocoons to go to the dark side any time during the hibernation.

The Creatures of Darkness, filled with both darkness and hate for anything bright or living, were growing in number and waiting for the time when life would reappear on Pangaea. They were able to break out of the protective Cocoon themselves, but when they tried to force open other Cocoons that were being protected, they could not break the seal. The exterior attacks on the protected Cocoons were always unsuccessful, and eventually, the Creatures of Darkness quit trying to open up the Cocoons that were encasing all life that was a part of the Good "Light" Magic.

Some of the Dark creatures that survived and grew in the Darkness were Gargoyles, unborn or newly born Erikings, and some of the unprotected dragons and dragon eggs. They evolved and were able to survive with the help of the Evil "Dark" Magic. Many other creatures that survived were consumed and transformed into Dark and Evil because they didn't have the protective Cocoons when the Evil struck Pangaea. The same is also true for those that lived in the surrounding oceans, especially those known as the Atlantians. The Atlantians were re-created by Hope the Fairie, who had also once trained and created the young Eriking, eventually called the Monarch King.

The Monarch King was the only creature who had been given a chance to open Pandora's Box. He learned and trained to attain the Magic trapped inside Pandora's Box. Millions and millions of years ago, when the King did open Pandora's Box, he chose to release only the Evil "Dark" side of Magic when he made his final decision.

The Atlantians were creatures that were used to serve both the young Eriking and Hope along with the other Fairies during the Monarch King's training in the middle of the Ocean. More importantly, both Erikings and Fairies were meat-eaters and the Atlantians were their only source of food during the time the young Monarch King was training to be a master of the Elemental Magic Power. Once all the training was complete, as they were all leaving the training grounds for the final time, as an act of Mercy or perhaps an act of Hate, Hope the Fairie, then known as "Evil," sunk the training grounds and the surviving Atlantians deep into the ocean. Naturally, both Hope and the Monarch King thought this would be the last of the Atlantians. However, the Atlantian's not only survived but they also thrived. The Atlantians were a race of highly intelligent creatures. With the power of science, they evolved and learned a lot more than Hope could ever dream of. Atlantis also survived the last act of the Monarch King despite that Lia the Canterpillar's protection did not reach it.

The Evil Darkness discovered life on Atlantis and grew there as well. The Evil lurked in the dark corners of the Earth, waiting for all life to awaken, so more battles could be fought between the "Good" and "Evil," "Light" and "Dark," and the Creatures of Darkness and those of the Light.

Chapter 2
Pandora's Box

To understand Magic, one must first understand Pandora's Box. The Pandora's Box is and has been the keeper of Magic, both the Good "Light" Magic and also the Evil "Dark" Magic. After all, Magic is much more complex than anyone realizes. Like day and night, it has two sides. It is either Good and made of Light or Evil and made of Darkness.

Pandora's Box was created when the galaxies first began. It has been around longer than any life as we know it. It is the keeper of Magic. It also has the job of transferring Magic where and when it is needed. When the time is right and it is time to move to the next Planet where life is beginning, the Pandora's Box will transport both the Good "Light" and Evil "Dark" Magic to their next destination when it is called upon by the forces of Magic, both Good and Evil.

Pandora's Box is also indestructible. It cannot be destroyed by any force or power. Even after the attack from the Darkness, it is intact and waiting for the moment when it will be time to awaken the world. The Pandora's Box is still several miles deep into the crust of the Earth, which has begun to separate Pangaea. It is still present deep inside the Earth. It will go where its next destination will take it when it is time or when it is summoned. The history of the Pandora's Box has been known to be on several planets in the past. A total of eight planets in distant galaxies have been the known visits of Pandora's Box. The Earth was the most recent of its destinations and t is still present deep in the Earth, several miles underground.

The planet where Pandora's Box had been before Earth was Atlantis, home to the Atlantians. It had also been at each of the home planets of the Original 6. Su the Pixie was one of the Original 6 who came across Pandora's Box on the planet, where all the Pixies lived and played.

This was the first planet that became home to Pandora's Box. It was called *Pixie*. Su's Planet, Pixie was filled with Light, Love, Goodness, and Kindness and was a very magical planet of the Light "Good" Magic. It was a planet with plenty of flowers, plants, trees, and lakes. It had wonderful weather. Life was in abundance on Pixie and all were truly happy and free spirits. It was a utopia filled with peace, love, happiness, and Good "Light" Magic. Su was the first to discover the Pandora's Box on her planet and thus was the Pixie that was first chosen by the Pandora's Box. Maybe that was a decision made by all magic or at least the Good "Light" Magic. Maybe Su made that decision herself. Perhaps all three of them had made this decision. Whoever or whatever was at play here, Su was the first of the Original 6 to see and touch the Pandora's Box. It was the first time that Pandora's Box had been seen by any living creature.

When Pandora's Box had first arrived at Pixie, it had been open and empty. From Pixie, the Pandora's Box scooped some of the Good "Light" Magic. For the first time ever, the Pandora's Box closed as Su the Pixie and the Pandora's Box moved on to their next adventure. When Su the Pixie moved to another world with the Pandora's Box, she became the first guardian, protector, and spokesperson for the Pandora's Box.

The second planet where Pandora's Box visited belonged to the Fairies and was known as *Fairie*. Fairies were dark creatures, but only a few were known as good. However, most of these were dark and truly evil creatures with little to no soul. After Su the Pixie, a male Fairie, Evi, discovered

Pandora's Box. Over time, Evi will come to be known as Evil when the young Eriking under his protection will release only the Dark side of Magic from Pandora's Box and become the Monarch King.

Evil was the same Fairie who betrayed the dark side and joined the forces of Good "Light" Magic. By wanting, seeking, and allowing the Good "Light" Magic to fill him up, he transformed from evil to good. And then, Evil was no more, and thus, Hope, the Fairie, was born. Although, in the distant future, Evil will be called Hope the Fairie, yet today there was only Evi.

Evi instantly accepted what Su was sharing with him and he became the second creature to join Su in watching and guarding the Pandora's Box. As Su and Evi began preparing to leave this world with the Pandora's Box, Su noticed that the Pandora's Box that had previously been glowing brightly because of the Good "Light" Magic it has taken from the Planet Pixie had now two compartments. The left one was *Light* while the right one was *Dark*. Even the area that had "Light" seemed to have dimmed down. This meant that Pandora's Box had taken Darkness and Evil from the Planet Fairie.

Su, Evi, and Pandora's Box landed on the third planet in their journey, called the "Unicorn" Planet. Z the Unicorn lived there. As they landed, Su noticed that the Pandora's Box had now more light as the Unicorn Planet was much like the Pixie Planet, filled with happiness, love, and Good "Light" Magic.

Su and Evi explained everything about their journey to Z the Unicorn, who joined them as another guardian of the Pandora's Box as the Pandora's Box glowed brighter due to the Good "Light" Magic of the Unicorn Planet that the box had now made a part of itself. Su, the Pixie, smiled when she saw that the Pandora's Box had gathered just as much light from the Unicorn Planet as it had gathered the Darkness from the Fairie Planet.

Su, Evi, and Z went to the fourth planet with Pandora's Box known as *Gargoyle*. This planet only had one ruler called *Dictator*. The Evil in this world was darker than the one in the world of Fairie. Here, Evi noticed that the light in the Pandora's Box had grown dimmer. He understood that Pandora's Box was storing the "Dark" Magic. As Evi practiced the "Dark" Magic, he knew he would be able to take it all from Pandora's Box when he finally released it.

He also knew that no one on the Gargoyle Planet practiced "Dark" Magic. It was just there, so when it would be released, only Evi will own it. He invited the Dictator on their journey, so the Darkness inside the Pandora's Box could increase.

Dictator was the only male Gargoyle on the Gargoyle Planet. He was the only one who had the ability to seed the eggs on the entire planet. If he were to leave the planet behind, no one else had the ability to seed eggs, and thus, the planet would eventually become extinct of the Gargoyle species and die as life on this planet would die too due to the absence of the only male Gargoyle, Dictator, who could seed eggs and reproduce their race.

Evi knew that, yet he invited Dictator with them. He didn't care that an entire planet would die because of his actions. He just wanted the "Dark" Magic that Dictator added to Pandora's Box. Evi told the Dictator he would be able to revive all his clan using the "Dark" Magic inside the Pandora's Box. Dictator agreed to become guardian to Pandora's Box. As the four guardians prepared to leave the Planet Gargoyle, Su the Pixie noticed that Darkness had almost completely filled up the Pandora's Box unlike before when they could see a balance of both the lights. Su the Pixie shared her concern with Z the Unicorn only. She and Z the Unicorn knew the importance of light and "Light" Magic.

The fifth World they went to was the Planet Yeti. The ruler of this planet was Emperor the Yeti. This planet was filled with happiness and harmony. It was similar to the Planets Pixie and Unicorn. At this planet, Pandora's Box filled up with light again, but it had not as much light as the Darkness. When Emperor the Yeti learned about the journey of the four guardians, he was excited to join them and hence agreed to protect the Pandora's Box.

In the Yeti Planet, Emperor the Yeti wasn't the only one who could reproduce. Other male Yeti could also reproduce fine without Emperor, so Emperor didn't need to stay at Planet Yeti. His clan would still continue to grow, even if he left the planet. Despite the fact that the Planet Yeti didn't have Magic, just like the Planet Gargoyle, it still had the light that brought brightness back to the Pandora's Box.

Emperor loved the Yetis and was known as a wonderful leader among his tribe and all of those that were known as Yeti. The Planet Yeti was warm and sunny, filled with wonderful and beautiful creatures that cherished love and harmony. It was a peaceful planet without any Darkness or Evil, unlike that of the Planet Gargoyle or that of the Planet Fairie. Emperor the Yeti didn't want to leave it at first, but when he was told to do that since he was the first to discover the Pandora's Box along with others. Su the Pixie, Evi the Fairie, Z the Unicorn, and Dictator the Gargoyle, Emperor the Yeti too had a future destined with it. Emperor the Yeti would only discover that if he accompanied them to the sixth planet as a guardian of the Pandora's Box.

As Emperor the Yeti joined the guardians, Evi and Dictator also began to sense and started to realize the changes in the light inside Pandora's Box. However, unlike Su and Z, Evi and Dictator didn't dwell too much as to why that was happening. The five, Su, Z, Evi, Dictator, and Emperor, along with Pandora's Box, were then taken to the next world in their journey. They arrived in the World with Dragons. This planet was known as the *Planet World Dragon*. This planet has three types of Dragons. First, Winged Dragons that were capable of Flight. Second, Land Dragons who could run at speeds that none of the other creatures from any of the worlds and planets could do. They were, in fact, the fastest running creatures in the entire galaxy. Then the planet had the Sea Dragons, who lived in the waters under the depths of the water. This was a planet like that of Gargoyle and Yeti. It didn't have any magic of its own, but it was filled with more light than dark.

On this planet, only the Alpha Dragon could seed the eggs. If the Alpha died, all the rest of the dragons would battle to become the Alpha that would seed the eggs. It didn't matter whether the winner was Land Alpha, Sea Alpha, or Winged Alpha. The most beautiful feature of the dragons was that some of them had only one head while others had two or three heads.

The Winged Alpha, the current Alpha of the Dragon World, was the sixth guardian of the Pandora's Box. When they offered him to joined them, he agreed and the light inside Pandora's Box became even. Both the light and dark in it were perfectly balanced with each other. The Pandora's Box had finally found the first six: Su the Pixie (Female), Hope the Fairie (Male), Z the Unicorn (Female), Dictator the Gargoyle (Male), Emperor the Yeti (Male), and now Alpha the Winged Dragon (Male). The Original 6 were chosen not only by the Pandora's Box but also by "Light" and "Dark" Magic.

After Pandora's Box chose the Original 6, it had found what it needed to move through the universe to worlds that did not have Magic but creatures that were just developing from primates. Pandora's Box had worked in the worlds that were still like an infant, just starting out. For instance, it went to Atlantis, which was destroyed because it chose the dark side of Magic. It is now buried in the ocean.

In the same way, Darkness was released on Pangaea when Pandora's Box was there. At this time, it is at the core of this Earth, which divided Pangaea into the seven continents of the world we live in right now: North America, South America, Africa, Antarctic, Australia, Europe, and Asia. The Pandora's Box might be older than time, yet it remained and managed to keep alive the Original 6 to this day, even if they had been severely injured during the war.

Pandora's Box is still a mystery and perhaps even more powerful than all of Magic. Who will be the next to discover it, even when it is buried deep into the Earth? Pandora's Box is now located where the deepest part of the ocean is now, and with life, soon all is about to resume and begin anew again. How long will Pandora's Box remain where it is? When will Pandora's Box leave to go to another planet and what will be the fate of all who live on the land and in the sea, if the Pandora's Box moves again?

Chapter 3
The Protected

All living creatures, even the plants both on the land and in the nearing oceans of Pangaea, were protected by the Magical Butterflies that Lia the Canterpillar released during the final battle. Yet, some of the creatures, those that were under the influence and power of the Evil "Dark" Magic, were able to escape from the protective cocoons if they decided to leave the protective cocoons by choice. In fact, every creature trapped inside the cocoons had the choice to leave them.

The ones belonging to the "Good" side knew that as long as they remained inside the cocoons, even if asleep, they would be protected from the forces of the "Evil" unleashed upon Pangaea on the last wish and command of the Monarch King. The creatures of the "Evil" sought the Darkness and willed themselves out of the cocoons, in the arms of the waiting Darkness. The pure of heart and the ones filled with goodness were in a deep sleep. Due to the goodness, they remained sealed in the protective cocoons. It would be a long hibernation for the purest at heart. They were to be awakened when the planet was safe again and life could grow again for all creatures, both Good and Evil. While the Darkness reigned in Pangaea, the Earth could not grow anything. There was no sunlight and so no nutrition was available for the creatures that needed it to flourish. Only after the Darkness was gone, the Earth could be fertile again for growing all things on Land and in the ocean. The creatures of the "Good" had to be in a deep sleep until the Earth was ready to sustain them again. The planet had to become capable of growing things from the ground again. This would include plants, grass, trees, shrubs, and even bushes. For living and breathing creatures of the land need food, and not all creatures are meat-eaters.

Many creatures only eat plants, grasses, or shrubs. For those that are Erikings, Fairies, Dragons, and even the Gargoyles to name a few are and always have been meat-eaters. They belong to the Dark Side, but they are not the only ones who eat meat. Many of the good creatures that are part of the furs and skins are also meat-eaters, but they are filled with goodness, especially if they were protected by the cocoons. If the cocoons released everyone before the planet could grow again, the creatures that eat plants would die a slow and painful death of starvation. For this reason, Lia the Canterpillar protected as much of the plant life on Pangaea as she could. She knew that the survival of everyone depended on the growth of plant life. If she hadn't, the Monarch King would have become successful in destroying Pangaea for good with the Darkness he had called upon it. Lia the Canterpillar's butterflies created the cocoons with the "Light" Magic from the Pandora's Box. They were designed in ways that would ensure the protection of all the life on Pangaea. They had mechanisms ensuring the safety of all creatures.

The cocoons protecting all creatures were such that they could not be opened from the outside. Their exterior could not be forced, dented, or opened in any other way possible for someone outside the cocoon. Such was its protection. Only the creature inside the cocoon could open it from the inside, with their strong willpower. The creatures filled with "Light" and goodness had no desire that they wanted to fulfill, and thus they slept peacefully inside the cocoons. The creatures of Darkness who had their desires to fulfill willingly opened the cocoons and lived in the Age of Darkness.

As the Darkness prevailed in Pangaea, the Age of Darkness let the creatures of Darkness roam freely. They grew in number as the Darkness recruited them and saved them from certain suffering. Lia the Canterpillar had intended to save all creatures whether they were Good or Evil. The Evil ones escaped the cocoons by will. The Good ones slept until the Earth was ready to grow again. This was the only way all life could survive and continue as intended. But that doesn't mean there was no life on Pangaea during the Age of Darkness. It existed in the creatures that belonged to the Dark Side of Magic.

At this time, the Darkness was free and protected those that were of Darkness and Evil. When the Darkness descended upon Pangaea upon the calling of the Monarch King, all that was left unprotected by the Butterfly cocoons, even if they belonged to the Dark side, had to suffer the wrath of the Darkness. Some creatures suffered for a few minutes and died very quickly. Others were not so fortunate and so they suffered for days and weeks. The Darkness that was present on Pangaea did not protect the suffering creatures. It gave the unprotected creatures two choices: submit to the Darkness and Evil summoned by the Monarch

King from the Evil of the entire universe or continue to suffer unprotected. The Evil from the entire universe found the environment of Pangaea conducive to its survival. However, it needed to grow. Therefore, the Evil needed creatures to submit to it. After that, the Darkness and Evil would fill the hearts of the ones who submitted completely. In this way, their hearts would become pure Evil, and no Light would ever find them.

The creatures of Light inside the cocoons were under the protection of Lia the Canterpillar. Evil could find no way inside the cocoons, so it only had those creatures to feast on, who had been left outside the cocoons. Evil offered the cocoons of Darkness to the creatures it protected from suffering. They were inside them as long as the Darkness lasted.

The Age of Darkness was all pitch-black Darkness on Earth. Any surviving life, Evil or Good, inside the cocoons now was made of both Light and Darkness. The creatures who didn't accept the Evil's offer and didn't die either transformed into Evil. This kind of Evil, in the Age of Darkness, was free in Pangaea. It did not need any vessel or leader to command it. It did need new hosts to fill their hearts with Evil and Darkness. However, all creatures Good or Evil trapped inside the cocoons by Lia the Canterpillar who willingly stayed inside the cocoons could not even be touched by the Evil lurking, just waiting outside. The Evil and Darkness could not open a single cocoon from the outside.

Lia the Canterpillar's plan worked for protecting life on Pangaea by creating an impenetrable fortress that the Earth remained for billions of years until it was ready to give birth to "Light" again and grow again so all who had survived would have means of sustaining their existence. The protection by Lia the Canterpillar remained intact for many years to come as the Earth took its time in rebuilding itself again.

Chapter 4
The Age of Darkness

The Age of Darkness began once the Evil forces were summoned by the Monarch King's final wish. Moments prior to the actual impact, Lia the Canterpillar and her trillions and trillions of Butterflies only had a few seconds to react. They did the very best to ensure that most would indeed be protected by the Magic of the Light, able to survive when the time would be right when the Age of Darkness was over.

Without any light, life as we know and living things couldn't survive, especially those that were filled with Light and Goodness. Without the Light of the sun, grass, plants, shrubs, and even trees would not grow. Without Light, the living creatures would suffer a faster rate of death and decay than any of the plants that live both on the land and in the sea. Not to mention, the entire planet was covered in Darkness and the Dust that was caused by the impact when the forces of "Evil" and Darkness struck the Pandora's Box. The Dust was so poisonous that if any creature or living thing breathed in it, they wouldn't survive without the help of Magic. It didn't matter if the Magic was of Good and Light or of Evil and Darkness. Only Magic could help creatures survive during the Age of Darkness. Only the creatures that didn't breathe air, such as creatures or living things that lived beneath the waters of the ocean. These were the creatures and living things capable of surviving, both with and without Magic.

There were some places where the Evil, the Dark Side of the Magic, was in total control. During the Age of Darkness, any creatures belonging to the "Good" and Light Side, who had been left unprotected without the protective cocoons, were easy to convert from the creatures of Good and Light to the creatures of "Evil" and Darkness.

The creatures who were already on the Dark Side were being protected by the Evil, so the Darkness could survive while those in the protective cocoons were hibernating. Any creature of "Good" and Light that had been left out of the cocoons provided by Lia the Canterpillar would have to turn to "Evil" in order to survive the suffering in the Age of Darkness. The creature of Light would first submit to the Evil, then offer themselves as a meal to a creature of the Darkness who were meat-eaters. Only through this process, could a creature of Goodness and Light transform into a creature of "Evil" Darkness. The creatures who were on the Dark Side always, such as the Erikings, Gargoyles, Dragons, and the Fairies, had the ability to survive during the Age of Darkness. They could live and keep the Evil, Dark Side of Magic, from becoming extinct. During the Age of Darkness the Erikings, Gargoyles, Dragons, Fairies, Winged Dragons, Land Dragons, Sea Dragons, the creatures of the deepest part of the ocean, the Atlantians, and any others that were not protected by the magical butterflies, who survived, were now a part of the "Evil" Dark Side of Magic.

Even the Dictator, the Gargoyle and the leader of all the Gargoyles, was not killed during the final battle. The Dictator's wings were torn off by the Monarch King, but he was left alive with the few of the oldest and the youngest of Gargoyles. The Dictator and some of his race managed to protect themselves by hiding inside a cavern as the war outside raged on. Soon after, even when the battles ended, they stayed trapped in the cavern. The cavern became home for the Gargoyle Clan for many years to come. They lived deep inside that cavern, which was always covered and protected by the Darkness.

Among all other creatures of the Darkness, the Gargoyles were affected the worst due to Light of Day. If the Light of Day touched any Gargoyle, they would immediately stiffen and turn into a stone statue. If Gargoyles remained in the sunlight for a long time, they would also die. The only thing remaining after them would be the stone statue only completely lifeless, with no hope of turning back to the Gargoyle form when it was night again.

Inside the cavern, the Gargoyles had another layer of protection. Years before the Gargoyles had occupied the cavern inside the deep dark cave, the Erikings had made their home there. They had also built a pyramid inside the cavern. Now that Gargoyles lived there, they had begun using the pyramid inside the cavern so they could have extra protection. The Erikings had lived outside together long before Magic arrived there. It was a time before Pandora's Box had traveled to all the different planets and acquired the "Light" and "Dark" Magic.

Soon the Monarch King would come to possess all the Darkness. Upon the last command of the Monarch King, when Evil and Darkness were summoned from all corners of the universe to Pangaea, Lia the Canterpillar used the Good

"Light" Magic in the Pandora's Box to summon trillions and trillions of Butterflies. These Butterflies covered all life on Pangaea that they could, but they could not penetrate the Pyramid and the Cavern. The Pyramid provided an extra layer of protection from the Light of Day to the Gargoyles, but it could not protect them from the Darkness as the Butterflies could not invade the cavern. As the Gargoyles were the creatures of Darkness, they survived it.

Dictator the Gargoyle, who had been through tremendous battle also survived, but he did not escape the war unscathed. He was injured and his wings had been ripped off his body. Even though the Dictator was now wingless, he had not lost the ability to seed the eggs of the female Gargoyles.

Dictator's wings were how the Gargoyle eggs became seeded. He, however, knew that he would not live for long, and the Gargoyle Clan needed a new Dictator who was not injured or weak like him. It was needed for the survival of the Gargoyle Clan. There was a way that would allow the Dictator to create a new Dictator. During the Age of Darkness, the Dictators survived on the available meat to regain some of his lost strength. He knew that meat was getting scarce as life on Pangaea was disappearing quickly.

Many had been enclosed in cocoons by Lia the Canterpillar and several had been engulfed by the Darkness and Dust. He couldn't leave his Clan without a strong and healthy leader any longer. Dictator knew that if he wanted to birth the new "Dictator," he would have to embrace death. When the time was right, he was willing to do that. Finally came the day when Dictator decided he was strong enough to create a new Dictator. He gathered his entire Clan about him that had been loyal to him and announced his intentions.

He told them that he was now a wingless Gargoyle and his time had come to an end. Upon his command, the female Gargoyles brought their eggs before him so he could seed them one last time and create a new Dictator to lead the Gargoyles. Dictator raised his hand. His sharp, talon-like nails protruded from his fingers. He thrust his hand into his ribs right below his heart.

As his Clan witnessed, his body trembled in unbearable pain, but he did not stop. The survival of his Clan was a lot more important to him than any pain he would have to bear for it. Before their very eyes, he pulled his heart out of his chest *which was still beating* and was barely attached to him. Dictator squeezed his heart and his blood poured over the eggs that had been brought to him. As his Clan saw, all his blood was absorbed by the eggs before them. Now they knew that one of these eggs would birth the next Dictator. His purpose fulfilled and his moment of strength now passed, Dictator fell back into his throne, breathless after drawing his very last breath.

Due to the Dictator's deed, the Age of Darkness had not seen the last of the Gargoyles. The Erikings, too, had survived the final battle on Pangaea. The Monarch King had acquired "Dark" Evil Magic from the Pandora's Box. With the help of this Magic, he had summoned all Evil and Darkness from the universe to Pangaea. The Monarch King knew he was dying, so he had used his last breath to *destroy Pangaea* for good. However, his plan had failed because of Lia the Canterpillar.

The battles had nearly killed all Erikings except the females who were pregnant or who had newly given birth *or survived the last battle*. The females in Erikings usually left the Clan and went away to give birth in isolation. Due to this, none of the female Erikings who were giving birth or who were expecting had been a part of the final battles. When Lia the Canterpillar had summoned Butterflies, the female

Erikings had been so far and out of reach. The Butterflies could not protect them. However, they gave birth to the new and young Erikings under the protection of Darkness. When the Monarch King had acquired "Dark" Evil Magic, the rest of the Erikings had gotten it as well. When Darkness and Evil from the universe drowned Pangaea, the female Erikings survived it with the help of the Magic they had. They were able to produce fresh meat using the Magic they had. They were also able to protect themselves from the Dust.

They turned themselves into creatures that did not need to breathe air to survive. As a result, they were protected from lethal Dust. In this manner, the Erikings stopped fearing the water as well. As they could survive without air, they knew they couldn't be drowned in the sea. The only weakness they had now was the soles of their feet. Their soles were soft and needed to be protected and covered at all times. Unlike the past, Erikings were now under the rule of a Female Eriking. She was known as "Matriarch," the Mother of all the Erikings. Matriarch was the oldest and also the strongest of all the remaining/surviving Erikings when the Monarch King took his last breath.

When the final battles ended, she had just given birth to four young Erikings. As Evil from the galaxy and the Dust began covering the entire planet, Matriarch knew that something was indeed very wrong. Instincts took over and she protected not only herself but also her four young newly-born Erikings. Other Eriking Mothers also did this instinctively. They all transformed with the Darkness of the Evil Magic so they could survive.

Yet it would take many years before any adult male Eriking would be mature enough to reproduce. Due to this, although Erikings grew in number during the Age of Darkness, they were still growing at a rather slower rate than before, at least when compared with the Gargoyle Clan. Other than the Gargoyle and the Eriking Clans, many other creatures of the Dark Side, such as the Dragons, Fairies, and the Furs also survived during the Age of Darkness.

Among these, one of the most prominent creatures was the Atlantians, who were living at the bottom of the ocean. They had arrived on Pangaea with the help of Evi the Fairie. They were creatures of the Darkness. After the final battles, most of the Atlantians had died. The few who had survived returned to the bottom of Atlantis.

When the Darkness and Dust hit the Pandora's Box, it was sent to the center of the Earth deep into the ocean where it stayed closed, filled with Darkness. The Atlantians at the bottom were also protected from the Dust and Darkness above the ocean surface and were able to survive the Age of Darkness. Although now the Atlantians are few in number, after a while, they will be among the most populated race on Earth after the millions of years when the Earth will finally begin to wake up.

In the Age of Darkness, Darkness and Evil grew and survived. The numbers of the creatures of Darkness became big and the creatures of Good and Light hibernated in a deep slumber. Somewhere inside, they all knew that when the Earth would heal and Light would emerge once more, the Good and Evil will be balanced again and a new battle will commence between the Light and Dark.

Chapter 5
The Original 6

The six consisted of Su the Pixie, Evi the Fairie, Z the Unicorn, Dictator the Gargoyle, Emperor the Yeti, and Alpha the Dragon, all in order from first to sixth. All six of them were the very first to learn of both Pandora's Box and were given a choice to use their free will. They could be a part of this adventure along with the heralds and protector of both Pandora's Box and the magical forces of Magic both Good "Light" and Evil "Dark" Magic.

The Original 6

Su the Pixie, a female from the Pixie Planet, was the first to find and be selected as a Protector and Ambassador for Pandora's Box. Su is the first of Pandora's and has been on this journey longer than any of the other five of the Original Six.

Su has been with Pandora's Box and is a creature filled with only Goodness and Love. Su has powerful Magic, Magic of the Good, and the side of "Light," and has the habit of only using it when it was absolutely necessary. She was born on Pixie a long time ago, and since then, she traveled with Pandora's Box as the other five joined.

Now, Su and her Magical Power increased, yet it remained as only that of Good "Light" Magic. All Pixies were beautiful, and Su held that beauty with a unique grace. She was small in stature and capable of both flight and teleportation. Their Magic extended beyond the years, being older than Pangaea and our entire galaxy.

Su believed in the power of the light, and being a creature filled with Goodness, she even cared for the creatures that were filled with Evil and Darkness. She would do anything to avoid battles and any loss of life, whether they were Good or Evil. After all, being a creature of the Light side of Magic, she had a pure heart filled with Goodness.

Over time, Su learned that, in order for Magic to be successful, it couldn't be limited to Evil and Darkness, as we had seen on the Gargoyle Planet many millions of years ago and, of course, considering what happened on the world known as Atlantis.

The once peaceful world lived in harmony until Darkness descended upon them. Suddenly, the home of Atlantians and the world that discovered the Pandora's Box were faced with the choice of Good and Evil, with only Evil that managed to prevail on their sight. They were thus beaten, slowly diminishing to nothingness as they chose the Darker side of Magic. It was just as the Monarch King chose the same path that of Evil and Darkness.

Regardless, Pangaea remained as the place which held balance and was filled with all types of life, unlike that of Atlantis. As compared to Pangaea, Atlantis was a planet where 95% of it was Dark and Evil while Pangaea was 64% Good "Light" side of Magic. This was all before the arrival of Pandora's Box and it left about 36% of the population as those being of the Evil "Dark" side of Magic.

Su was now in a deep stage of hibernation and was oblivious to what happened to both Pangaea and those who were not protected by the Good and Light of the Butterflies from Lia the Canterpillar during the age of Darkness.

Evi the Fairie, also known as "Evi," was commanded by the Monarch King to have his name changed to Evil. Instead, he turned against the Monarch King and joined the side of the Good, the "Light" Magic, to transform into "Hope." Evi came from a world that is only known as "Fairie." His home was much like the other worlds, and it too was filled with more Darkness and Evil rather than Light and Goodness. However, Su the Pixie and Z the Unicorn's homes were the only ones whose Home World was filled with only that of Light and Goodness. Dictator the Gargoyle's home planet shared the same fate as Evi the Fairie and was filled with Darkness and Evil.

Evi, being the Fairie that discovered Pandora's Box, was known as the chosen, but it was still unclear whether or not it was fate. It was the same case for all of the other five of the Original 6; Su, Hope, Z, Emperor, and Alpha. Evi was always the one with the most powerful Magic, yet his planet was certainly more mischievous than Evil and the darker side was greater overall – 70% darkness and 30% light. Fairies were known to be cruel creatures and used the Magic they possessed to do evil things to others. This was especially the case when it came to mating. After all, the Fairies' ego was very powerful and it fueled the Darkness inside a large number of them.

They knew their power and held pride in their kind, often proving it by bringing down those who were not as great as them. Chaos would often ensue with the Darkness as they rose to bully the weaker Fairies, just to exert their power. They enjoyed bringing misery to less fortunate Fairies or those that were of the Good and the "Light" Side of Magic.

However, it was said that a Fairie had a tendency to change over time from Evil to Light or Light to Evil. Their actions were responsible for the shape of the future and for the choice they would all make individually of their free will. If they did good things, then they would gain the light of Goodness.

The more they focused on doing good and shared it with others, the more they would be filled with Goodness and Light. It was also true for the Evil or the "Darkness" of Evil. It was all about how much they focused on their power and practiced. If it focused on the Dark or the Evil side of Magic, they would only end up becoming the worst version of themselves.

As we all know, Evi is now only known as Hope and he was the one who had experienced all the sides, both the Good and "Light," and also that of the Evil and "Darkness" of Magic far greater than any of the other five – Su the Pixie, Z the Unicorn, Dictator the Gargoyle, Emperor the Yeti, and Alpha the Dragon. Hope had used his experiences and chose to become Hope ever since he turned against the Monarch King. There is no more Evil, but only Hope.

Z the Unicorn was a mystical creature filled with The Good "Light" magic. Prior to the arrival of Pandora's Box on her planet, it had always been filled with only that of Goodness and "Light." The unicorns on her planet bore the same Goodness and it was easily seen that there was no Evil, nor Darkness. No amount of Evil and violence that she got to witness fazed her from her Goodness, and she stayed true to it over the millions of years that she had been with Pandora's Box.

There were many times that she often thought of hopefully, someday, being able to go back to her home planet of Unicorn. However, while it may sometimes be challenging, she knew what they are doing is much greater than her personal desires and thoughts.

If there was anything that plagued her mind, it was the thought that if the forces of Magic were not Balanced, then the future could turn toward a much more Evil. The "Dark" side of Magic could eventually become very powerful. The Power would be enough that it, the Evil, could once again return to Z's homeworld.

Eventually, it could destroy her home planet as the Evil once did on the world known as Atlantis. The fear and incessant need to protect her world had followed her since she first became part of the Original Six.

Dictator the Gargoyle and his other Gargoyles were all from the Planet Gargoyle, which was only filled with Darkness and Evil at all times. It was a world where the light was never seen at any time. Not only did Gargoyles live in this world, but other creatures of Darkness also did. Yet, the planet was controlled by the Gargoyles and none other. They were the creatures known to inflict pain or death on other Gargoyles. It was only the Dictator who was the most advanced and the strongest and who stood as the first atop all other Gargoyles. He was also the only one capable of seeding the Gargoyle eggs for future generations.

When Dictator left his home planet with Pandora's Box and the others, he knew that his species on the Planet of Gargoyle would soon die off and, over time, cease to exist. It was only a matter of time. But it didn't bother him, for the darkest of the dark side of Magic had other plans for him and it had ensured it when the time was right that the Evil, "Dark" side of Magic had the ability to create an abundance of

Gargoyle eggs for Dictator to seed and ensure that his species would again grow in both populations. They would ensure that they would not only survive but also manage to become even more powerful when the time was right. The difference between a Male Gargoyle was that all of them had Wings and the ability to fly. On the other hand, the females didn't have wings and thus could not fly on their own. While it was all the males who had wings, it was only the Dictator who stood out and remained unique. Only he had the ability to seed the unseeded Gargoyle eggs.

When fresh, unseeded Gargoyle eggs are created, Dictator will fly over them, and from the lower part of the interior and exterior of his wing, a dark mist will begin to form. Slowly, the mist will spread over the eggs and eventually seed all of the new eggs.

Gargoyles didn't have any other abilities. It was only the Evil, "Dark" Magic, which would keep Dictator alive over time. The circumstances were all noted and prepared for. In the event that Dictator would become injured, it was the Evil, "Dark" Magic, which would keep him ageless and strong, never keeping him in jeopardy of failing.

Dictator knew that all he had to do was to remove his

black, beating heart from his chest with his clawed arm and then squeeze it as his last living act. The blood would pour over several unseeded gargoyle eggs and only one would rise to ensure that another future "Dictator" would be born to keep the Gargoyle in existence and build a future. After all, Gargoyles could only live in the Darkness. The Light was their weakness. It had the ability to kill the Gargoyles. It kept those creatures in that state, ensuring them to be part of the Darkness and ensure the Evil and chaos of the dark side of Magic.

It was this same Magic that protected Dictator as he has traveled from planet to planet with or without Light and Darkness. He had gained the strength to continue on his path and eventually live up to his name as the greatest 'Dictator.'

Then came Emperor, who had been the leader of the Yetis for a long time. There were a lot of things separating Yetis from Dragons and Gargoyles. The first was that they were all capable of reproducing on their own, unlike Gargoyles or Dragons. Secondly, they were filled with far more Goodness and Light than that of Evil or Darkness. They were simple creatures and physically very powerful. But they did not have any type of magical power. They had a greater sense when it came to seeing in day or light. They could also smell other creatures, as well as their own kind from many miles away. However, it wasn't only their noses that were powerful, but they also had powerful hearing abilities, unlike most other creatures.

Yetis were certainly filled with far more Goodness and Light than that of Evil or Darkness. However, there were two things that would take away Yetis' Goodness:

1. Food shortage: They always preferred to maintain a vegetarian diet, yet in certain cases, they would also eat meat if they did not have any plant-based food sources.

2. Mating season: When it was time to reproduce and if the Male Yetis were far greater in population than that of the mature, reproducing females, then this could create problems for Yeti. After all, they were more than animals. It was the instinctive side for all Yeti. However, when the reproduction was done, they had plenty of plant food available.

Otherwise, the Yeti was carefree and peaceful, both with other Yetis and other creatures. While they were similar to the Gargoyles, they didn't have any type of Magical Power or control over any magic. Alpha the Dragon was the sixth and final member of the Original Six and was from the Planet Dragon. What was astonishing was that it was not a magical place. Yet, it had both Light and Darkness. It was a place where all types of dragons had lived and ruled since the beginning of the time of this world. It was home to the Winged, Land, and Sea Dragons. It had both land and ocean and sun for the light of the day. Not only that, but it also had darkness for the nights. It was not a magical place, but it held a major similarity to Pangaea.

As Alpha had agreed to be the sixth of the Original 6, he managed to learn the Power of Magic when the time was right. It was that Magic that would eventually create Dragon Eggs for Alpha to seed when the time was right. Alphas breathe fire, which was deadly to most creatures. The fire that Alpha can create is different than all the other Dragons. The type of fire that comes from Alpha's mouth differs a lot. The first fire is of death and destruction when hunting or fighting. The second fire concerns seeding the unseeded dragon eggs when the Magic created the dragon eggs on Pangaea many years ago. When talking about eggs, there were also two distinct eggs that were produced from the first batch of magically produced dragon eggs. Those two were the ones that would eventually give birth to the other two Dragon Alphas. In essence, they would belong to the Land Dragon Alpha and then the Sea Dragon Alpha.

Once these other two Land and Sea Alpha dragons came of age of maturity, it was only then that they would be responsible for seeding the other Land and Sea Dragon Eggs. Amongst them were Winged Alpha, who would continue to seed the Winged Dragon eggs. In all of the Original 6, the reproduction of Dragons would eventually have Alphas, which would be capable of reproducing on their own.

Dragons were also similar to Gargoyles and Yetis, for they, like Gargoyles and Yetis, did not possess nor control any type of Magic. The question was, were the Original Sixxx chosen, was it by chance or planned in advance by Pandora's Box and the two sides of Magic, or perhaps was it a sheer incident taken place by chance? After all, a balance of both Good and Evil Magic had traveled from one planet to another. There was only one and the only planet to end tragically and to be replaced by that of Evil and Darkness. That was the World of Atlantis. Pangaea was on a similar fate, but because of those of Pangaea and also because of Su,

Hope, Z, Emperor, and the Alphas. Pangaea had a fighting chance to become whole and would, one day, be ready for all life to live and be whole again.

The Pandora's Box, still on Pangaea, included the hibernating protective cocoons from the Good Side of Magic. It also included those who were capable of living in the Age of Darkness during hibernation. Pandora's Box would remain in Pangaea, even though it was in the deepest part of the ocean floor at this time.

For the first time, Pandora's Box remained in Pangaea far longer than any of the other planets it had traveled before arriving in Pangaea. Now because of the Original Six, life had a chance. Soon, it would have both life and light, which would allow all living things to have the necessities of life.

Chapter 6
The New 6

Pangaea's battle took place to give all living things a chance to defeat the Eriking Monarch King before he destroyed all life in the world. It was Su the Pixie, Z the Unicorn, and Hope the Fairie that gathered all the living creatures who were not Erikings or Gargoyles. Of all those present at this gathering, sixteen (16) candidates were initially chosen as those filled with the Good "Light" Magic and who had hearts filled with only love and goodness.

Some creatures were part of the Fur Clans, then from the feather clans, animals from the Skin Clans, then from the Scale Clans, and then, of course, from the Fin Clans. All of them were present at this gathering when the selection for the champions would be determined. It was decided that, from all these various clans, as well as those in attendance, only sixteen would be chosen as champions. The selected would be worthy to free the Good, the "Light" side of magic which was trapped for millions of years in Pandora's Box. For the most Evil of all the Eriking's Monarch King during those millions of years of the Good, the "Light" side of magic was still trapped in Pandora's Box and under his control. Those sixteen chosen would finally free the Good Side of magic, which was trapped in Pandora's Box. From the Fur Clan, Bo the Male Bear, Lea the Female Lion, Q the male Squirrel, Wu the Male Wolf, Tay the Female Tiger, and X the Male Fox were chosen from the Fur Clans like the champions and part of the sixteen.

Those selected next were creatures from the Feathers Clan. They were Dy the Male Duck, Mac the Male Macow, and O the Male Owl. The next champions were those from the Skin Clans, Ele the Female Elephant, Liz the Female Lizard, and Ri the Male Rhino.

The Scale Clans were represented by Lia the Female Canterpillar, Pi the Female Spider, and Ty the Male Toad as the Scale Clans' Champions. Tay the Female Turtle was the only selected from those of the Fin Clans. After all, most of the Fins required the water of either the surrounding Ocean of Pangaea or a large lake on Pangaea. Tay was a creature who could live on land and not need water at all times, which is why she was amongst the chosen. The final selection for the sixteen champions was the one and the only creature not from Pangaea. Instead, it was Z the Female Unicorn who was also the only one of the Original Six selected to be part of this new group of the sixteen champions. As the battles continued, blood raged amongst good and evil, filling the lands. Finally, when the war was over, only six of them survived. It was a dark day with the survivors sitting dark amongst their lost friends. From the Fur Clan, Q the Male Squirrel survived. From the Skin Clan, it was Liz the Lizard. From the Scale Clan, it was Ty the Toad and Pi the Spider. From the Fin Clan, it was Tay the Turtle.

Then there was the last of the six who survived. There were Z the Female Unicorn and Lia the Canterpillar part of the Scale Clan. The one who freed the Trapped Magic in Pandora's Box. However, Lia the Canterpillar had transformed into trillions of Butterflies who used the Good "Light" Magic to protect all living creatures.

They did that by creating the Protective Cocoons, ensuring that life would again, one day, come out of the protective hibernation and allow all living things and the entire world of Pangaea to sustain once again. After all, before Lia's last act of creating the butterflies, it was said that they were never seen. With the Good, the "Light" Magic was finally set free and able to grow.

What would or did happen to Lia? Was she alive or did she transform into something else? Did Lia sacrifice herself to save all of those she loved and cared about to ensure that life would have a chance to continue?

All we now know is that the Original Six contained Su the Female Pixie, Hope the Male Fairie, Z the Female Unicorn, Dictator the Male Gargoyle, Emperor the Male Yeti, and Alpha the Male Dragon. With the Original Six and now the New 6, only Z the Unicorn was chosen. Only in the past was it possible that Magic or Pandora's Box was selecting those to be a part of Magic and Pandora's Box.

When the Original Six were chosen, it was a balance of both Good "Light" Magic and that of the Evil "Dark" side of Magic. However, for the New 6, it was filled with only those who were a part of the Good, the "Light" side of magic. It would require that the New Six be only creatures filled with both the Light and Goodness to join and save not only the entire Pangaea but also our entire galaxy. What only a few knew was that the reason this happened was that it was the Eriking Monarch King's final act. He had summoned all the Evil not just in our world and galaxy, but the entire universe to destroy all of Pangaea.

In order for all to survive, including Pandora's Box, the New Six was created, especially since both sides of Magic were free and neither the Evil nor the Good Magic was trapped. Magic was aware that, during the Age of Darkness, it would be Evil that was in control. After all, no light from the sun could shine on Pangaea.

None of the air is breathable, and there was no plant that would be able to grow without sun or air. Life is present, yet all experience is either in a protective Cocoon or the Good "Light" Magic. While those of the Evil and Darkness side of Magic even the survivors were filled with Evil and Darkness, it would take time for a new balance to happen for both Pangaea and Magic eventually. That was why the New Six were only those from the Light Side of Magic.

When the day of being released from the Protective Cocoons came, those in the Cocoons would one day wake to see that Evil did survive. Again, it would mean Good versus Evil. Light against Darkness would be too, as it had in the past, be at odds for the fate of all living things.

Pandora's Box had been around since before the beginning of time and would be around long after all the universe would be no more. It would react to ensure that this would happen until the end of time. That is why the New Six, the survivors of the Champion 16, were protected in the suspension of the protective Cocoons. It was highly unlikely that Z the Unicorn, Q the Squirrel, Liz the Lizard, Ty the Toad, Pi the Spider, or Tay the Turtle were aware that they were the New Six for both Pandora's Box and Magic.

Chapter 7
Liz the Lizard

Liz, the Female Lizard, was born originally as a member of the Skin Clan. At the time of her birth, the Skin Clan was one of the lowest clans. The Skin Clan, like the other lower clans: Fur, Feather, Scale, Fin, and Skin Clans, was at the bottom. No creature had given any of these clans much thought before. After all, when Liz was born, the Ruling Clan at the time of her birth was the Eriking Clan. The Erikings led by the Monarch King were second to none in terms of both ranking and power.

During the time of Pangaea, there were well over 6,000 different Lizards species. Liz, as a young lizard, would spend most of her day basking in the sun. Needing the sun to heat a lizard's body was very important. As the world was during the Age of Darkness, the rays could not penetrate into Pangaea's surface since the dust from the last attack of the Monarch King. Lia's Butterflies protected Liz and most of the other lizards and other lesser-known species of life. Lizards then made use of their senses of sight, touch, and hearing, like other vertebrates.

Lizards were mainly carnivorous, often being sit-and-wait predators. Many smaller species ate insects. Many species relied on hearing for early warning of predators and essential resources, which included basking, feeding, and nesting sites, as well as refuge from predators and fleeing at the slightest sound.

Liz had what was known as a perceptiveness personality. This was because of her senses and ability to explore and be vigilant for others. She was not at all afraid of any task that was requested or required. Being a creature of the light was the reason why Liz was the chosen one. Necessary resources included basking, feeding, and nesting sites, as well as refugees from predators.

The habitat of the species affected the territories' structure. For example, rock lizards had settlements atop rocky outcrops. Some species may aggregate in groups, enhancing vigilance and lessening predation risk for individuals, particularly juveniles. Liz had both excellent hearing and eyesight. It was these that allowed her to save countless other lizards. She also saved creatures from all the lower clans and even those that were not even clan-worthy. With many other clans, which were far more powerful or significant than any of the lower clans "Fur, Feather, Fin, Scale, or Skin," Liz the female Lizard, being a part of the Skin clan, was never thought to be powerful or even feared by any other clan. Erikings, Fairies, Gargoyles, Dragons, and even Yetis existed at the time of Liz's birth and upbringing. This was also true for all the other lower clans and creatures that didn't belong to any clan. Liz had loving parents, along with many siblings. Being a lizard, it was a life to survive. It was able to hide in various locations such as a forest or the swampland of the desert.

Most lizards were not sought out since they were small creatures. It took a lot of energy for the higher, meat-eating clans to capture most lizards. When they were caught, those lizards were more often nothing but a tiny snack. So most of the higher clans that were meat-eating creatures did not even seek out lizards. Yet, one clan did enjoy eating lizards, which was the Fairies' Clan. Since all Fairies were not large in stature, any lizard caught or captured by a Fairie would indeed be a large meal and quite tasty. Even the skin of the Lizard was not enough for the Erikings to use to make foot coverings for the highly sensitive soles of their feet. Thus, when a Fairie captured a lizard, that Fairie could eat the entire lizard and not worry about saving the skin for the Erikings. Like most of the other lizards, Liz lived moment by moment, trying to survive and being able to live another day in the world of Pangaea.

Liz was chosen for what she had done in the past before she was selected as one of the New Six. Liz, at times, put herself in direct danger to ensure that not only other lizards, or even other Skins, all lower life such as Fairies were near or seeking Lizard or any other meat.

Liz always warned and saved many other lower clan creatures from not only the Fairies but also the Erikings, Gargoyles, and the Young Dragons. After all, a Young Eriking, a Young Gargoyle, and even Young Dragons were like Fairies. They were all meat-eating creatures from these clans. Liz faced the fairies many times and saved an untold amount of lower creatures from being their next meal.

Liz's heart was only matched by the goodness and also being one in the face of her darkest, scariest fears instead of just saving herself. She would save many other creatures when in the face of danger, leading to being killed. These Heroic acts and being so brave put her life in danger countless times.

Liz was only filled with light and goodness. This was why she was chosen as part of the 16. Liz and the others, those of the New Six: Z the Unicorn, Q the Squirrel, Ty the Toad, Pi the Spider, and Tay the Turtle were unaware that they were chosen to be the New Six. Soon, as they all awakened, the Age of Darkness had passed. They would have more challenges and many events in which they would all play a significant role.

Chapter 8
Pi the Spider

Pi, the Spider, also a member of the New 6, was born and raised on Pangaea. Spiders ranged in size from the tiny Samoan moss spider, which was .011 inches long, to the massive Goliath bird eater, a tarantula with a leg span of almost one foot. Pi was, by no means before magic, the largest species. Neither was she the smallest species of Spider on Pangaea. Most species were carnivorous, either trapping flies and other insects in their webs or hunting them down. They couldn't swallow their food, though spiders did inject their prey with digestive fluids, then sucked out the liquefied remains.

Though not all spiders would build webs, every species did produce silk. They used the robust and flexible protein fiber for many different purposes to climb (think Spider-Man), to tether themselves for safety in case of a fall, to create egg sacs, to wrap up prey, to make nests, and more. Most spider species had eight eyes, though some had six. Despite all of those eyes, many didn't see very well. A notable exception was the jumping spider, which could see more colors than humans. Using filters that sat in front of cells in their eyes, the day-hunting jumping spider could see in the red spectrum, green spectrum, and UV light. Pi had been blessed with eight eyes and could jump great distances and produce silk. Being a member of the Scale clan on Pangaea helped both Pi and the other Spiders to continue to live. After all, Erikings, Fairies, Gargoyles, and even dragons had no desire to eat any spider.

Pi had a personality known as intuitiveness. Intuitive was an interior sense of danger or events that are currently happening. This made Pi very valuable during times of battle or even when meeting new creatures for the first time. Pi, more often than not, always trusted her intuition. Thus, they were not hunted as they had little to no meat and were not sought out by those in the higher clans.

It was yet a part of the Scale clan when they and the others, "Fur, Feather, Skin, and Fin Clans," were all called together. Pi wished to do her part to help all living creatures and keep Pangaea safe for all life. Pi was chosen for her goodness and as a follower of the light. What separated Pi from the others was that she was not afraid to sacrifice her life for others. She had little fear by the standards of Pangaea had little power, and most creatures did not fear or even think twice of any spider. While growing up, she was initially in the Gargoyle territory, the place that gave her birth. It was only when she was mature that she was ready to go out into the world of Pangaea on her own, like the others who were mature and ready to leave the only home they had known.

They all would wait for a strong gust of wind to blow them to wherever they might end up. Pi ended up with no other Spiders and Scales members, yet she found comfort and those that she would call friends and family in the outskirts of what is known as the Yeti territory.

Pi, when was at the Yeti territory, helped a young female Yeti that was pregnant and about to give birth to a Dragon that was hunting this young pregnant Yeti. If Pi did not bite this dragon in the eye as she did, it was highly doubtful that the Young Yeti would have had a chance to survive. But because Pi's act against a creature was a million times bigger and stronger, a full-grown land dragon saved Yeti. However, with this heroic act and by saving the young mother to be, she also saved the four offspring that she delivered within minutes after Pi had stunk the eye of the Land Dragon. Pi, with the Goodness and the "Light," kept putting herself in front of others. Even though she was unaware that she had been selected to be one of the New Six. Also, Pi had eight eyes with sharp eyesight and she was able to see in both the day and night time and climb things that others could not.

Pi could even create webbing or build nests when needed or required along with the fact that all of the higher clans "Erikings, Fairies, Gargoyles, Dragons, and Yeti" do not pay any attention to a creature such as Pi since she, in their eyes, was just a spider. An advantage for Pi and those of the light, by being overlooked, was that she could at any time in most situations be easy to investigate and crawl in places where others of the "Light" may not be able to, for they were far larger than Pi.

With the Magic of the Good and the "Light," Pi became the most powerful of all the Spiders and is a fierce warrior. If she was afraid of any creature, she never showed it. Due to her love for both Light and Life, she was a protector of those that cannot protect themselves. Pi, like Liz the Lizard, because of their size and appearance, was a new part of the New Six. Even though they were all unaware, it would be essential when they all awakened from the time known as "The Age of Darkness." After all, the protective cocoons' time to end was certainly closer every passing moment.

Chapter 9
Q the Squirrel

Squirrels were members of the family Sciurid – a family that included small or medium-size rodents. The squirrel family included tree squirrels, ground squirrels, chipmunks, marmots, flying squirrels, and prairie dogs.

For Q, he was a ground squirrel with exceptional climbing skills. If needed, Q could enter Prairie Dogs' tunnels beneath Pangaea's ground as well. This allowed him, other Squirrels, as well as other members of the fur and the lower clans to hide in these tunnels during a hunt. The Fairies enjoyed eating any type of Squirrel. They found that the raw meat from a Squirrel was delicious as a snack or meal if several squirrels were caught and captured.

Q was also born and raised on Pangaea throughout his life. He was one of the first 16 champions. He was both a survivor of the last war and had also been held in a safe protective cocoon, like many other squirrels, furs, feathers, skins, and scales. The smallest squirrel was the African pygmy squirrel. It grew to 2.8 to 5 inches (7 to 13 centimeters) in length and weighed just 0.35 ounces (10 grams). The Indian giant squirrel was the world's largest known squirrel. It grew to 36 inches. Q and other squirrels ate nuts, leaves, roots, seeds, and other plants. They also caught and ate small animals such as insects and Canterpillars. These small mammals were always wary of predators because they were tasty morsels with few natural defenses. Sometimes, groups of ground squirrels worked together to warn each other of approaching danger with a whistling call.

Q had what is called a logical personality. He was very wise and always thought before reacting to anything. He was highly intelligent and not quick to make decisions in most situations. Squirrels are terrific climbers and come to the ground in search of fare such as nuts, acorns, berries, and flowers. They also ate bark, eggs, and baby birds. Tree sap was a delicacy to some species. Whether they dwelled high in a tree or an underground burrow, female squirrels typically gave birth to two to eight offspring. Babies were blind and dependent on their mothers for two or three months. Mothers may have several litters in a year, so most squirrel populations were robust. Like other rodents, squirrels had four front teeth that never stopped growing, so they didn't wear down from the constant gnawing. Tree squirrels were commonly recognized and often seen gracefully scampering and leaping from branch to branch. Other species are ground squirrels that live in burrow or tunnel systems, where some hibernate during the winter season. A group of squirrels was called a scurry or dray. They were very territorial and would fight to the death to defend their area. Mother squirrels were the most vicious when protecting their babies.

This was how Q had gained his reputation for he had, more times than can be counted, defended the mothers and the helpless baby squirrels when they were under attack. Q, being of what was known as an Indian Giant Squirrel, had his entire life been sought out by both Fairies and even young Erikings; Dragons and Gargoyles to be their next meal. Q was highly intelligent and highly adaptable. It was no wonder that Q and many other squirrels had been able to survive. For the longest time, Q had a reputation as being both highly intelligent and competent. He could feel fear, and when he did, it drove him to have his heightened senses: smell, vibration, sight, and hearing. Yet, when the battle happened, he shrugged off that fear and became a fierce and mighty warrior. Q had been known for he had often been involved in many heroic acts of saving not only other squirrels along with other Fur's. He had extended help to all creatures that were of the Good and the "Light."

Because of all that Q had done as a new member of the New Six when he awoke from the "Age of Darkness," he would have new adventures and many things that he and the others would face as the new age of Pangaea was about to happen.

Chapter 10
Tay the Turtle

Turtles are reptiles with hard shells that protect them from predators. They are among the oldest and most primitive group of reptiles, having evolved millions of years ago. Turtles live all over the world in almost every type of climate. Turtles spend most of their lives in water. They are adapted for aquatic life, with webbed feet or flippers and a streamlined body. Sea turtles rarely leave the ocean, except to lay eggs in the sand. Freshwater turtles live in ponds and lakes and climb out of the water onto logs or rocks to bask in the warm sun.

Tortoises are land animals. Their feet are round and stumpy, adapted for walking on land. They dig burrows with their strong forelimbs and slip underground when the sun gets too hot. Turtles live on land and in water, usually in swamps, ponds, lakes, and rivers. As for Tay the Turtle, she is a Freshwater Turtle and was born and raised on Pangaea her entire life. Tay is the type of turtle who can retract her head and feet into her shell. That is how Tay was able to sneak into the Eriking territory where Pandora's Box was held under the watchful eye of the Eriking Monarch King. Tay has an introverted personality, as are all the turtles. However, she showed that she, even when afraid, would rise and do what was requested to help the others. As we all know, when the Erikings were sleeping, she began to make her way toward Pandora's Box. Once the Monarch King started to wake up, she retracted her head and feet, tricking the Monarch King and the Erikings into believing that she was a stone and not a living creature.

Tay and other turtles have shells around them divided into two parts: the top (carapace) and the bottom (plastron). The carapace and plastron are bony structures that usually join one another along each side of the body, creating a rigid skeletal box. This box is composed of bone and cartilage. Because the shell is an integral part of the body, the turtle cannot exit it and neither the shell sheds like the skin of some other reptiles.

All the turtle's senses are well-developed and are used in avoiding predators and finding and capturing food. Their eyes have the typical anatomy of any vertebrate having a good vision. Aquatic turtles have eyes that can quickly adjust to aerial and aquatic views, seeing well in both situations.

This natural defense is what kept Tay alive throughout her life, especially during the last battle in the Monarch King's home. It was the territory of the Erikings when the Champion 16 were attempting to free the captured Good "Light" Magic which was being held trapped in Pandora's Box. Most turtles are active during the day, spending their time foraging for food. They all also lay eggs but need to find a place on land to lay their eggs. Usually, they dig a nest into the sand or dirt and then walk away. No species of turtle nurture their young babies.

What a turtle eats depends on the environment it lives in. Land-dwelling turtles munch on beetles, fruits, and grass, whereas sea dwellers gobble everything from algae to squid and jellyfish. Turtles reach the age to mate at different times. Some come of age as young as a few years old, while others don't reach sexual maturity until around 50 years have passed. Turtles are *amniotes*. They breathe air and lay their eggs on land, although many species live in or around water. These cold-blooded creatures have an incredibly long life span. Turtles are not social creatures. While they typically don't mind if there are other turtles around them, they don't interact or socialize.

Unlike other turtles, Tay was extremely social and enjoyed having the company of not only turtles or other fins but also all types of creatures. Even though Turtles were not known for being brave or warriors, at times during the mating season, male turtles would, indeed, battle other male turtles for the right to reproduce. However, for Tay, she had been protecting and putting herself in jeopardy numerous times to protect other creatures.

Tay was chosen as the one and only member of the Fin Clan who was part of the 16 Champions. Her bravery, social attitude, and will to risk her life for others made her part of the New Six.

Chapter 12
Ty the Toad

Ty the Toad is a member of the Scale Clan like Lia the Canterpillar and Pi the Spider. Ty is the bravest toad in the Scale Clan. He is one of the 16 Champions born and raised on Pangaea. Just like others, he was chosen because of his bravery. Ty, when he was born, was like most toads. He enjoyed living near the water in one of the lakes on Pangaea. Toads were typically not eaten by Fairies, and if a Fairie ate any toad, they would become infected with warts all over their entire body.

Ty has what is known as a perceiving personality and often relies on what he sees, hears, and smells. He relies on his perceiving ability and exerts himself to find a way when things begin to go wrong.

As for the other Higher Clans that ate fresh meat, Erikings, Gargoyles, and even Dragons did not find any Toad meat filling. Toads were in abundance on any lake in Pangaea that had warm or hot weather.

Toads are amphibians, which means they are capable of

surviving without water if required. However, for them to persist in abundance, water allows a greater success rate for survival. This survival instinct made Toads different than the other higher, more powerful clans that were more likely to be hunted for a meal. Toads often ate any living thing that would fit in their mouth, including bugs, spiders, worms, slugs, larvae, and even small fish. To catch prey, their sticky tongues would dart from their mouth and pull the prey into their mouth. A toad's tongue can snap back into its mouth within 15/100ths of a second that often doesn't give a chance to the prey to escape.

For enjoyment and to seek vengeance, Fairies would hunt and kill toads in the Scale Clan sometimes, especially when any Fairie was infected from warts due to direct contact with a toad. The wart infection was contagious, similar to a cold. It could spread out to the other non-infected healthy Fairies upon contact. The approach of the Fairies here was to ensure the safety of the other Fairies. For the Fairies, this was the only creature on Pangaea that could without intentions, harm or infect other Fairies. Ty, the Toad, was the first to realize this and upon this discovery, he instantly became the most well-known Toad in all of Pangaea. He would often feel pride that made the other toads think that he was brash and arrogant. However, Ty, since his birth, had always been a part of the Good, the "Light" Side. His heart was filled with love and concern for all creatures of the Light Side of Pangaea. Like most Toads, he did not fear anything since they were not a species that was hunted for food.

After Toads found out what they could do to Fairies, they knew that if they were to see any Fairie, they would either have to hop on that Fairie and have direct contact or use their tongue to touch a Fairies' exposed skin. Once that happened, the Fairie would instantly create chaos, so great that the Fairie would instantly teleport away from where it just happened.

Fairies knew that if any of the other Fairies found out about this accident, they would report this to the other Fairies that would result in their instant destruction to ensure the safety of the other Fairies. Since a toad's tongue can attack and retract within 15/100th of a second and most Fairies were capable of teleporting even faster than that, it would require an element of surprise for a Toad to be successful and not to be seen or found anywhere near the Fairies. Ty the Toad was without a doubt the one toad who had, before being one of the Chosen 16, infected more Fairies than any other Toad along with the fact that he was and had always been the bravest of all the toads. After all, it took a great deal of confidence for any toad to attempt to come into contact with any fairie.

Ty, before being one of the 16 Champions, had infected many Fairies. This included the ones tortured by Evil Fairies. Ty, during one of those encounters, infected 16 Fairies at one location within 20 minutes and created a feat. Any other toad in the clan hadn't defied this as of yet.

Like all toads, Ty is comfortable in the water, near water, and on the land. Since the Erikings feared the water, the only natural predator from the higher clans had always been the Fairies since the day "Evil" and the other Original Six first arrived.

This is why Ty was chosen as part of the 16 and now had been selected as a New Six. This was once his hibernation was over and the protective cocoon freed Ty and all the Toads. Significantly, the vast majority of the Fairies changed sides, stopped serving the Erikings, and joined our heroes during those last few battles to end the terror of the Monarch King and his Evil, "Dark" Magic.

Chapter 13
Z the Unicorn

Z the Unicorn was the only one who was part of both the Original Six, which included Su the Pixie, "Hope/Evil/Evi" the Fairie, Dictator the Gargoyle, Alpha the Dragon, and Emperor the Yeti. Z the Unicorn was also the only one of the Original Six who was chosen by the Good, the "Light" Side of Magic. She would be a part of the New Six once the Cocoons were no longer needed or required. She was the first and the only leader of all the species on her home Planet, "Unicorn."

Z's home planet is truly a Utopia, for there is no Evil and Darkness. It is a bright and beautiful world that is filled with both happiness and love. The Unicorn World also has plenty of Magic, all of which is of the Good "Light" side of Magic.

There is no hate, anger, jealousy, rage, nor any type of Evil in the World of Unicorn. Z was when she first visited Pandora's Box with Su the Pixie and Evi the Fairie before deciding to be part of the Original Six. Z is a mighty member of the "Light" and has always been a part of the Light since she first arrived. Z has the personality of what is known as the Protector. Z always has been very protective of all creatures of the Light. Instead, she was created as new flowers bloom since they were both very magical places filled with harmony and happiness, of course, all under the Good, the "Light" side of Magic. Z was, without a doubt, the most powerful of all mystical and magical creatures from her home planet.

As we know when the Young Eriking, who would later be known as the Eriking's Monarch King, released the Evil, the "Dark" side of Magic, it was millions of years before any other Unicorn or even Pixies would be created.

After all the Good, the "Light" side of Magic had been trapped and because it was trapped and held prisoner by the Monarch King, the *light* side of Magic was not capable of growing. Without any Good "Light" Magical growth meant no new Pixies or even Unicorn would be created.

Z was one of the last of a handful that had survived when the Unicorn population started to shrink to less than 500 Unicorns total in all of Pangaea after all Unicorn meat was by far the most sought out and desired by the Erikings.

The Monarch King would only eat unicorn. For this was by far the one meat that he loved second to no other type of fresh meat on all of Pangaea. Z, with the help of Magic, has lived for millions of years and to this day she looks very young and is quite healthy and very powerful in both Good Magic and Light, which also happened to be very powerful physically.

She has a heart of Gold and never intentionally hurts any creature that is of the Good, the "Light" side. Z helps and assists anyone if she can, even the ones who call her their enemy. However, the fate of the entire world or planet is under peril of death, doom, and destruction of all life and living things. Z during events such as that can and would become one of the fiercest, a deadly warrior for the Light. Z, also being a creature that was born on a Magical Planet "Unicorn," has known of Magic and the Good, the "Light" of Magic her entire life.

She has always been well-loved by those of the Light regardless of clan or ranking. Z ranked the creatures based on whether they were a part of the Light. After all, Z has spent the last several million years on Pangaea under the Evil and Darkness during the time of the Monarch Kings that ruled. Z saw thousands and thousands of her species (other unicorns) hunted, killed, and then eaten by either the Monarch King or another Eriking.

Z was, without a doubt, the one Unicorn that the Monarch King had wished was killed. He desired more than any other unicorn to be the one whom he feasts on. Yet, he is no more. Z has evaded and escaped and was one of the primary creatures that helped to free the Good, the "Light" side of Magic from Pandora's Box with the others.

Unlike all the other creatures that were still being protected in the Magical Cocoons created by Lia and her butterflies, Z is capable of *knowing* what is going on in Pangaea during the "Age of Darkness."

Z, along with both, Su the Pixie and the Fairie now known as "Hope," were the only three magical beings *who knew* what was happening. They continued not only to survive but also to increase their population and grow much stronger *from* the Evil, the "Dark" side of Magic in all of Pangaea.

Z the Unicorn, Su the Pixie, and the Fairie have and do continue to share with themselves the events that happen and keep communication between the three of them magically.

For they all know, Pangaea is nearly healed and would again in the very near future be able to sustain life, living creatures, and also be abundant in both plants, blades of grass, and shrubs. That the air would be clean and breathable. The water which has been poisoned by the Evil, "Dark" magic could be made to good freshwater.

After all, one of the Magical Powers which Z and any other Unicorn had was to make a body of poisoned water *into clean safe water*. Just having the Magical horn on her head dipped into the contaminated water to become fresh to purify it, so all the living creatures would be able to drink without suffering any death or agony.

Since the Darkness, the Evil has been the only thing since the day of the Cocoons, with Pangaea needing millions of years to heal and recover. Places, where others were sleeping, would wake up and would not be aware that these former water holes, those that before the events were safe and clean water.

Only to be filled with Poison and Evil to take away the life from the Light, Z is aware that she and those other new unicorns that were created on the day that Good, the "Light" side of Magic were set free. When the time to be released and freed from the Protective Magical Cocoons came, she and the other Unicorns would immediately have to visit all those areas where the poisoned water was waiting for an unsuspecting creature of the Light to seek out water to drink.

Z, Su, and Hope also knew that the three of them would have many tasks and things to accomplish to ensure that those whom Lia's butterflies protected for millions of years would be required because all of the land-based creatures of Pangaea would immediately *require* fresh, clean water to ensure they could live a long and healthy life.

Z would be the leader of the New Six which would include Q the Squirrel, Liz the Lizard, Ty the Toad, Pi the Spider, and Tay the Turtle. This would be the second group with Pandora's Box and when it would be time to travel to another planet when that time eventually comes. These would be the Six Guardians of Pandora's Box and Z would be the leader.

One thing that Pandora's Box would do much differently than it did before when it first started with Su the Pixie being the first creature *contacted* by Pandora's Box. In Su's group of the *Original 6*, all the other members were from distant and different planets and worlds. Yet with the New Six, the five new members were all born and raised on Pangaea and Z would be the only from a different world. Was this because of the Good, the "Light" side of Magic being trapped, yet freed? Or something else? For the Age of Darkness was nearing the end, soon the Light of day would again shine, and shortly after that, those who were in the protective cocoons would be freed to pursue life again and live in a world without the ruthless, Evil Monarch King of the Erikings.

Chapter 14
'Atlantis'

Pandora's Box's first journey was to Su the Pixies world. Next was "Evi-Hope" the Fairies world. Then it was to Z the Unicorn Planet and next was to Dictator on Planet Gargoyle, followed by Alpha the Dragon and then to Yeti World, home of the Emperor. These were the first six places where Pandora's Box traveled first to select the Original Six. However, the seventh planet was known as Atlantis, home of the Atlantians.

Atlantis was the world that was visited before Pangaea, and like Pangaea, the ruler of the Atlantians was a woman named "Atla." She was, in many ways, just as dark and ruthless as the Monarch King. She only chose to release the Evil the "Dark" Side of Magic in Pandora's Box, unlike Pangaea, that was saved because the Good, the "Light" Side of Magic, was eventually freed. The World Atlantis did survive and because the Evil and Darkness were so great, the entire planet eventually became impossible for any life to exist. It wasn't long before the whole planet of Atlantis became entirely extinct and no more or even any signs that a world had been where Atlantis once was at. Pandora's Box, before the destruction of Atlantis, took the Original Six to the World of Pangaea, where it was from the start during the Monarch King's young days when he was still just a Young Eriking. The Young Eriking needed to learn Magic's future craft like Atla on the Planet Atlantis had to. Since Erikings were significantly less intelligent than any other Atlantian, it made Atlantians far superior to any other species, at least science and technology-wise.

The Young Eriking was stuck with his apprentice training in a secluded place, decided by Evi the Fairie, Su the Pixie, and Z the Unicorn. Evi the Fairie looked and thought to himself that perhaps it would be best to keep the young Eriking's attention by having the Magical Training continue in an isolated location. Since Pangaea had all the landmasses connected into one giant landmass, it was nearly impossible to find a place where the young Eriking's training could continue in seclusion. That is when Evi, with the blessing of both Su and Z, decided it would be best to use Magic to create a place in the middle of the surrounding oceans of Pangaea. It was a place that would not be connected to Pangaea, instead of a sole mass of land similar to what would later be known as an island. With the Magic of all three, Su, Z, and Evi, they created a place named Atlantis. Since both the Young Eriking and the Fairies would need fresh meat, Evi created the Atlantians as well that had only two purposes. The first was to serve both the Young Eriking and the Fairies. The second was to provide both of them with fresh meat to ensure that they could survive by having constant fresh meat. When the day arrived when the Young Eriking had completed all the training for Magic, Evi, and the other Fairies as they departed from the place they had named Atlantis, they decided to sink the landmass deep into the ocean.

They all thought this would be the end of the Atlantians. However, as we learned, the Atlantians survived. They also transformed into creatures who looked similar to men. But unlike men, they could live in the depths of deepest oceans and even on the land. They also had superior technology. Instead of Magic, they pursued science and advanced in areas more advanced than anything and anyone had ever seen on all of Pangaea. Atlantians were generally around 8-10 feet tall and had a slender built. They were physically powerful and highly intelligent compared to all life on

Pangaea. Only the Erikings with the Magic could easily defeat them. Even the Gargoyles and Dragons were physically much stronger than any of the Atlantian. However, since Atlantians had advanced technology, they would have the upper hand. In the last battle against the Erikings, on Pangaea's surface, they were easily defeated by the Erikings because they controlled "Gargoyles and Dragons."

Like all wars and battles, some of the Atlantians did survive. They immediately went back into the ocean and returned to the home they lived in since it was sunk into the deepest depths of the ocean. However, when the last act of Evil summoned all the Evil of the Galaxy, Dark Magic, with the last dying breath of the Monarch King, it first started to strike Pandora's Box.

With such a force that the power sent Pandora's Box deep into the crust of the landmass on Pangaea. The force was so powerful that what others had thought or assumed was strong and powerful enough to destroy Pandora's Box. Yet Pandora's Box didn't get destroyed. Instead, it was sent several miles deep. During the "Age of Darkness" and as time passed, Pangaea was beginning to separate into several different continents where the Evil was summoned and struck, the center of Pandora's Box. That place had become the deepest part of the ocean in the entire planet of Pangaea. It was so deep that only Atlantians or Sea Dragons could travel there.

The Sea Dragons had no desire for Magic and weren't curious whenever they saw Pandora's Box in the depths of the ocean. They would often continue doing what they were doing and never gave what they just saw a second thought. However, when a group of the Atlantians first founded Pandora's Box, they were creatures with high intelligence and decided to take Pandora's Box back to the place they all called Atlantis.

Naturally, Pandora's Box had been closed since the strike of the Evil. This was summoned by the Evil Monarch King to destroy all life. Good "Light" and Evil "Dark Magic" both Atla and the Monarch King decided to keep the Good, the "Light" Magic trapped. This time, Pandora's Box was sealed and filled with the darkest of Darkness – the evilest and vilest type of Magic. Just as it was in the past, it would require someone to open Pandora's Box, and now that Pandora's Box has been taken to the Atlantis, it would be an

Atlantian who would eventually set it free the darkest of dark Magic. Another event was that Lia's butterflies did not even know of Atlantis' existence. Because of that, Atlantis was taken over by Evil, the Darkness in the depths of the ocean where it is pitch black and cold.

Soon, it would be a matter of time when life on Pangaea would again be back because the Age of Darkness was nearly at the end. The Age of Darkness would reoccur when Pandora's Box would be opened with a more significant, far more vicious force and filled with only the Evil, the Darkest of Dark Magic, along with the help of science and technology never seen before.

The Atlantians started to explore the surface, and much to their surprise, they noticed all the cocoons. Even with their technology and equipment, they could not break open any of Lia's magical cocoons. When they attempted to lift or even move the cocoons, they could not because of the Good, the Light Magic. However, this made their visits to the surface quite frequent.

The Atlantians learned that other Evil, Dark Creatures that were not protected also survived. Since the planet was covered entirely in Darkness, the Gargoyles would be out at all times. After all, they had grown in population since the last war.

The Erikings, who were noticed by the Atlantians, saw that they had grown in population and were no longer ruled by the Monarch King. But they still feared the Erikings, for they did have both powerful Magic and Strength. These newly evolved Atlantians would be far more potent than any creature except for Erikings, Gargoyles, and Dragons. They had plans to be the ruler of all of Pangaea's land and the water. Soon, they would seek revenge on Pangaea's surface, even when the single landmass would begin to separate into several different continents.

Chapter 15
'Old Enemies, New Allies'

It was only a matter of time when Atlantians would come into direct contact with either Erikings, Gargoyles, Dragons, or one of the transformed creatures because of the Evil, the "Dark" magic on the land of Pangaea.

The first contact between the Atlantians and one of the surface dwellers was a young female Gargoyle. The Atlantians noticed that all of the creatures on the surface were typically very thin in built. After all, the food was scarce and the fresh meat was not in abundance as it was in the past. In the depths of the surrounding ocean of Pangaea, much fresh meat and plenty of sea creatures were available on which the Atlantians could rely.

Instead of fighting to the death, a member of the Atlantians offered the Female Gargoyle some fresh meat. When the female Gargoyle saw the fresh meat, she could think of only one thing - FOOD! Fresh food and plenty of fresh meat. As the young female Gargoyle was quickly eating the fresh meat, the Atlantian began to speak to her,

"Gargoyle, as you can see, we Atlantians have plenty of fresh meat. We have enough fresh meat to feed all Gargoyles for a lifetime."

The young Gargoyle, as she just finished her fulfilling meal, looked over at the Atlantian and responded, "What is it that you will need from me, Atlantian?"

The Atlantian responded, "I wish to meet with the Gargoyle leader and will bring enough fresh meat for all your species to present as a gift for making an introduction to your leader."

The young female Gargoyle responded, "Dictator is our leader."

"I know of your leader Dictator. Take me to him."

"No, you do not know the Dictator, Atlantian. The Dictator you know of had died a long time ago. This Dictator is not the same Dictator you know of," said the Gargoyle.

After all, the original Dictator made sure that his species would survive and tore out his beating heart with his own hands. He squeezed it and seeded the Gargoyle egg to ensure that the future Dictator would be born to lead all the Gargoyles. Since so much had passed, this would be the one who the Atlantian would need to meet. It was agreed upon by both of them. The young female Gargoyle and the Atlantian began to enter the cave where most of the Gargoyles lived.

The Dictator was in front of all the other Gargoyles and spoke, "Who is this creature that you have brought us, young female? Is it fresh meat for your leader?"

The Atlantian kneeled to show respect to the Dictator and replied, "No, Dictator, I am not your meal today. And if I am, then how will I bring you and all these other Gargoyles meat? Looking at all of your Gargoyles, it appears to me that you all are starving."

The Atlantian could see with his own eyes how thin all the Gargoyles were and knew that from his earlier experience with the Young Female Gargoyle that her species was struggling to have enough fresh meat.

"Then, where is all this fresh meat? I do not see any meat except for the meat on you!" Dictator replied.

"I can take you to where the meat is and give you all that you can eat and also all that you can return with for your clan if you wish," responded the Atlantian.

The Dictator agreed and thought if the Atlantian were not honest, the Dictator would eat the Atlantian. The Dictator began to flap his mighty wings and picked up the Atlantian to the pitch-black sky in flight.

"Tell me, Atlantian, where are we going for all that fresh meat?" He asked.

"Take me to where the land meets water and then wait for me on the shore so I can return with plenty of fresh meat, Dictator," replied the Atlantian.

While the Dictator agreed, he wondered what would happen if the Atlantian tricked him. As time passed, the Dictator was about to return to the cave. It was then that the Atlantian, with the others, began to exit from the ocean. The Dictator also saw that they all carried as much meat as they could.

An Eriking who was hiding saw what had happened. At first, the Eriking thought to join the Gargoyle. After all, every Eriking had Elemental Magical powers and was far physically stronger than any the Gargoyle or Atlantian. However, since they were few, the Erikings remained hidden from Pangaea's others during the Dark Ages. There was one

Eriking alone and there was just one Gargoyle and many Atlantians, more than enough to kill the Eriking. The Eriking decided, even with hunger telling to attack, to remain hidden and just listen and watch.

Dictator agreed that if the Atlantians would continue to supply plenty of fresh meat to all the Gargoyle Clan, then it was decided that the Atlantians could do two things. The first was to be allowed that all the Atlantians could travel to any parts of Pangaea and not be attacked by any of the Gargoyles. The second was "IF" they needed help or were to be attacked, then the Gargoyles would be on their side when the Age of Darkness was over and be loyal to the Atlantians. The Dictator immediately agreed to these terms, and thus this was the beginning of two former foes who were known to be allies. This helped the Evil's side, the "Darkest" Side of Magic, to grow with this new alliance.

With the dawn of a new era and as the Age of Darkness was beginning to come to an end, the Atlantians knew that soon another war was to start because all the protective cocoons would open and a new life would begin.

Chapter 16
Man

As the Age of Darkness's final days began to end, the Pangaea healed and was ready for new life and light. But how could the balance of "Good-Evil, Light-Darkness" be maintained without the other? After millions of years of being in the protective cocoons, which were nearly ready to be opened, changes happened. It wasn't only on the surface and outside the protective cocoons but also inside the cocoons, for certain species that were beginning to be awakened had transformed.

There would be no more dinosaurs that once ruled the lands of Pangaea long before there was ever the Monarch King. After all, the dinosaurs were the first species to become extinct because of the Erikings who ate them all for fresh meat and used their skins to make coverings for their sensitive feet. The new species had evolved and grown in both population and appearance. Pangaea, which was once a singular mass (one continent), now was divided into seven different landmasses, which were slowly drifting apart. The most significant change was a new species that had evolved.

This new species would later be known as "Man." Before man, there was a species that was known as plant-eaters. These ancestors did not have higher brain functionality and were not even classified as any clan.

As the cocoons began to open, there was plenty of evidence that these new creatures that we know as 'man' would be called *Neanderthal*. The other species would later be known as Homo Sapiens. Homo Sapiens had a much greater intelligence than the Neanderthals and would eventually evolve to be known as what we all call 'Man.'

For all the others exiting from their long hibernation, the most significant change that was seen was the lands of Pangaea. The other was these two new species: *Neanderthals* and *Homo Sapiens*. What side of Magic would they serve and be a part of? Would they choose the Light or the Darkness and what role would they have shortly? After all, this was not the end of the time known as "The Age of Darkness." It was also when the Evil, the Darkness, which had continued all this time, was to end. A new era, a new age was to take place. The period that the Darkness of the Atlantians and the Gargoyles along with those who serve them have been waiting for. Next will determine the fate of not only all of this world but the entire galaxy.

Find out soon.

Pangaea: The Origin of Magic Volume 4, "The Atlantians."

ROGER SCHAFER

www.ingramcontent.com/pod-product-compliance
Lightning Source LLC
Chambersburg PA
CBHW052012170626
46808CB00007B/2893